# Lesbian Erotica Sex Stories for Women

## Lesbian Sex Short Stories, Extremely Bisexual Hardcore Erotic Rough Dirtiest Collection, Romance, BDSM, MMF And More.

Sasha Coleman

# COPYRIGHT

publisher. The information herein is offered for informational purposes solely and is universal as so. The presentation of the information is without contract or any type of guarantee assurance.

# Contents

# *Inflight entertainment*

Another long intercontinental flight, this time with rather arduous connections. I had been flying from Ireland to Istanbul for almost 4 hours to continue towards Zimbabwe. Back and forth across the time zones meant that I had to change trains at half past one in the morning. I felt wheeled and had already watched most of the films I was interested in on the outward flight. Half an hour in the back gates at Istanbul Airport was just enough to tip a quick beer, then my flight was called.

I was one of the last to squeeze into the waiting bus when I noticed two young women who had made room for me. They definitely looked Asian, maybe Central Asian or North Chinese, I couldn't really judge that, but since I was standing directly behind one of them, I was amazed to find that they spoke Russian. Strange.

They were by no means classic beauties, their features were a bit too edgy for that, and yet they had something when they spoke to each other excitedly and energetically. Her animated facial expressions and her bright laughter were a pleasant ray of hope, and I watched them discreetly. They were similar, but didn't seem to be sisters. Both were very slim and petite, one almost as tall as me, the other almost a head smaller. They were dressed quite youthfully, an eclectic, urban street style - the little one with her back to me had put a trucker cap over her long, silky hair. She was wearing a very loose-fitting, gray shirt that left the left shoulder free so that I could see the wearer of a black lace bra on her flawless, tanned skin.

Well, shortly afterwards all the passengers were sitting in their seats, and I just couldn't see any of the two. I installed myself and got ready for an uncomfortable night. I looked around me and, somewhat resigned, I realized that the crew on board didn't give much in my aisle. But then I saw a delightful stewardess in the other aisle, which made me suddenly forget my dissatisfaction and tiredness. Truly a sweet creature. She had tied her blonde (probably bleached but tastefully done) into an elegant knot on the back of her head. Deep brown almond eyes sat over a pretty snub nose, including very sensual, full lips that released pearl white teeth when smiling. Long-limbed, elegant hands, with soft pink lacquered nails. But above all, her uniform gave full breasts under the tight jacket, and a well-rounded butt under the pants. Too bad that she had shift in the right aisle, but I smiled kindly across the middle rows, which she replied with a friendly, professional smile and nod.

The usual announcements, security procedures, and the start, and then we were in the air. The meal was soon served and I was delighted to find that the blonde stewardess had landed in my passage. So I peered forward along the aisle and watched with joy as she bent and stretched in front of the service car. When I got there I gave her my most charming smile and when she handed me my mug, our fingers brushed at random. That was the greatest feeling, after all, an entire Airbus had to be operated. But I had just seen on her name tag that her name was Sahida. And so the trays were cleared again, the lights were dimmed, and all the passengers gradually set themselves up to sleep.

Then I saw the two girls from earlier that had got up and were doing a little stretching a little further forward before going to bed. Quite smooth the two … Lunge with springs, bend the upper body sideways and forward, and then especially the back stretch in the hollow cross. First there was the big one, which turned to her side, her upper body bent 90 degrees forward over the side of the seat, and then the back was pushed right through, rocking her small, tight butt back and forth very easily. Then lewd thoughts came to me. Then it was the turn of the little girl to stretch her legs, which brought  her delicate bonds to good use. The big one gently massaged her shoulders. I didn't hear anything from the distance but her delightful expression spoke volumes. I would also like to have the two of them kneaded, I thought …

My neighbor was already asleep and I must have been completely immersed in the sight; I was slightly excited and felt a gentle tug in the crotch. I involuntarily spread my legs a little and adjusted my hangers a little. Then a pink fingernail ran gently over my upper arm … I looked up in amazement and looked into Sahida's dark eyes, which eyed me suspiciously; a slight, somewhat mocking smile played on her lips. "Well, is it getting a little too tight for you here?" She asked. I replied, with an ostensibly neutral tone, that the seats actually offer relatively little legroom, but at the same time I looked at them with undisguised pleasure. 'Then maybe you should stretch your legs a little further back in the machine,' she suggested, stepping forward a little,

I didn't hesitate long, got up and walked slowly and quietly down the hall. Sahida followed me towards the rear galley. Once there, I was waiting for them. She was already there and pointed conspiratorially to the third toilet cubicle, which was designated as a cubicle for the disabled. We looked around briefly - everything calmly - then we slid silently into the toilet one after the other. Sahida locked the door behind her back and looked at me defiantly.

I came close to her and gently stroked her cheek with my hand. What tender skin! Then I grabbed her by the side of my neck with a firm grip, and my lower jaw with my thumb, and kissed her. Her lips opened and a curious tip of a tongue ran briefly between my lips. It tasted delicious, a seductive scent of cinnamon and ripe peaches. Her whole body seemed to nestle against mine, and I felt her plump breasts press against my chest. I bravely unbuttoned her jacket and grabbed her around the waist with her left hand and her chest with my right, where I stroked her breast with my thumb through the white shirt and bra. She was probably only wearing a thin bra, because I felt her nipple stretching curiously towards me. 'You villain, you,' she said,

She rubbed her crotch against mine, and felt my already plump masculinity through the layers of fabric. 'Oooh,' let out a soft moan. She stepped back and looked down, then expertly ran a flat hand over the bulge in my pants. She cooed contentedly. We both got a little impatient and unbuttoned each other's shirts. She stripped off her jacket and shirt, and the sight of her plump, light brown breasts in a white lace bra made my mouth water. She gently stroked my chest hair and palpated my firm pectoral muscles as I freed her treasures from her prison. Shapely and heavy, her beautiful, plump breasts stood proudly over her gently rounded, flat stomach, crowned by dark areolas from which the nipples protruded stiffly. I gently weighed my breasts in my hands, then leaned down to pay my respects with my mouth and tongue. I felt Sahida's knees give way, and a sigh of pleasure escaped her throat.

I fiddled with her trouser button, then slipped off my troublesome trousers. She was wearing white lace panties that contrasted most appetizingly with her brown skin. I touched her ass with an enjoyable grip - what magnificent, firm, well-rounded hemispheres! I massaged the firm ass flesh and felt Sahid's excitement increase. Suspicious heat emanated from her lap and the moisture of your vagina penetrated clearly through her panties. On the lower legs, however, she was still affected by her pants. I  didn't want to take her off completely - the cabin floor wasn't that clean, and she still had half a shift in front of her. I brushed off her panties and ran my fingers gently over her vagina, over which a neatly trimmed landing strip stood. It was soaking wet and acknowledged my touch with lustful moans. Impatiently she tugged on my pants now, brushed off my pants and panties so that my strap, freed from the tightness, now proudly stood in her direction. She licked her lips expectantly.

I didn't want to torch for much longer. We had remained undiscovered so far (maybe Sahida and her colleagues had a deal there too), but other night-walking passengers might be wondering why the cabin was occupied for so long. So I turned her away from me and motioned for her to rest on the edge of the sink with my hands. Her wonderful ass stuck out from under the hem of the shirt and pinned me expectantly. I started my spanking on her swollen, juicy, shiny plum, pulled my acorn briefly through the slit to moisten it, and then thrust into her cunt in a sweeping train. Sahida gasped and gasped for a moment. It was tight, soaking wet and scorching hot. 'Oooh ... big' sighed Sahida,

Now I started pushing into her with long, gentle strokes. She bucked at me with every push and slowly began to moan softly. Her magic cunt nestled around my shaft like a velvet case. Every centimeter was a delight - from when I passed her greedy labia with my thick, swollen acorn deep into her, where my helmet made hidden parts sound inside. I grabbed her by the bells and gently massaged her full breasts. Sahida had her head back and was completely committed to our rhythm.

Our excitement rose slowly but surely, and I put on a tooth: faster and firmer I pushed into her willing cunt, so that with each push my heavy balls slapped her behind. She whimpered and with every thrust a suppressed 'yes', 'fuck', 'more' escaped her ... man was the little horny. I felt my balls slowly contract; soon I would be shot down. Then I pulled out of her. She groaned in disappointment and looked over my shoulder questioningly: 'Go on, you can, it's safe ...' I turned her back to me and motioned for her to pull a leg out of her pants and panties, and then sit on the edge of the sink. It was a somewhat precarious situation because the edge was not wide enough to sit really stable, and there was not enough room towards the back to support yourself properly. I told her to lean my head against the mirror, then went down on my knees and grabbed her two thighs just above the knee, then lifted them up to my chest level.

Sahida was now stuck between me and the cabin wall like a folding knife, and her cunt gaped towards me at the level of the pool. In fact, her hip was slightly above mine now. So I started my spanking again and pushed into her willing hole. Her cunt smacked eagerly and Sahida rolled her eyes because I was pushing her from below, and because of the unfamiliar position her semen channel was even tighter than usual. The lower tip of her cunt was the most delicious on the underside of my shaft and the sensations were so intense for both of us that we couldn't wait any longer.

I now slammed into her uncontrollably. Sahida had surrendered entirely to her feelings and let herself be willingly nudged through. Her mouth was eagerly open and her legs clung to my back. Her breath went into a steady moan and I felt her close to the climax. I leaned back a little to increase the butt angle and felt the inside of my cock rub inside against the abdominal wall over a very sensitive  area. Sahida cried out choked and spurred me on to pick up speed. My eggs boiled over and I felt the sentence rise inside me. Sahida's cunt twitched as it climaxed, and I poured myself into it in large, fiery bursts. She literally milked me.

We both slowly came to our senses. She kissed me deeply and sensually: 'you son of a bitch, you ...' I carefully took some paper towels which I put on them as I pulled out so as not to stain our clothes. We straightened up and looked at each other with a conspiratorial expression as she pushed the bolt back and we sneaked back into the dark cabin. She gave me another kiss when she disappeared down the hall. I was about to slide back into my seat when I saw the smaller of the two girls I was watching coming back from the back of the plane by the toilet cubicles and gave me a mischievously amused look ... Had she heard everything?

The End.

# *The last guests*

Although Laura and Gregor had been living in this area for several months, they had never noticed the small corner restaurant. It was a small, nice restaurant, which apparently was well cooked, but where people from the neighborhood also met for a good beer.

The two wanted to have a bite to eat and so they sat down at the small table by the window. That evening all the tables were taken and a group of men were sitting at the bar.

Everything in this little inn was extremely good. The waitress read the guests' every wish, the food was excellent and the atmosphere was cozy and pleasant. The visitors at the other tables talked animatedly, the waitress chatted and laughed with everyone, and the group was engrossed in a cheerful conversation.

Laura and Gregor enjoyed the evening. Because they liked it so much they stayed, talked and drank on. They liked the whole atmosphere so much that they didn't notice how the shop was slowly emptying. After a while only she and the group were there at the bar. They ordered another drink and continued talking.

The men from the bar slowly left the shop. Finally, only a 50-year-old gentleman sat at the counter and talked animatedly with the waitress. While they talked like this, they looked at the young couple at the small table by the window. After a while the gentleman got up and went to Laura and Gregor. He introduced himself politely to them as Werner and then sat down at their table without asking  for their permission. With a wave of his hand, he gestured to the waitress to bring another round.

Werner started to ask them about their lives, they talked about their time in the city and their job, but also about various other things.

After a while Gregor apologized to go to the bathroom. No sooner had he left the table than Werner turned his gaze to Laura unceremoniously, eyed her plump breasts that pressed against her T-shirt. After looking at her silently for a few moments, he asked her to get up. Laura was confused, irritated by the look and the request, but not shocked or worried. Without thinking about it she got up. "Turn around" asked Werner, Laura obeyed and Werner looked at her crispy ass with relish. "Sit down before your friend comes back" and as she sat he added with a smile "you little bitch." What had the man just said? why had she obeyed him at all? Laura looked Werner in the face, perplexed, but this did not seem to be in the least unsettled.

Before Laura could answer Gregor was back and at that moment Werner got up and said goodbye. Laura was now barely able to utter a sentence, she was too confused and shocked by the man's words, but also by the tingling that caused this situation in her abdomen.

A little later they paid and left.

Laura didn't tell Gregor a word about what the stranger had said to her in this restaurant and although the whole visit had been extremely nice until then, she decided never to go back to that restaurant.

A few weeks later Laura was in the cinema with her two friends Anja and Julia. After going to the cinema they wanted to go out for a meal and because Gregor had talked so enthusiastically about this little corner bar, they finally persuaded Laura to go there. She couldn't and didn't want to tell her friends about the experiences with Werner. When they entered the bar Laura was filled with a mixture of fear and excitement and when she found out that Werner was not in the bar she felt less relief than disappointment.

The three sat down at an empty table and ordered from the friendly waitress who had already served Laura and Gregor. They ate and drank, talked and Laura had almost forgotten the encounter the last time she opened the front door and three men entered the bar. To see the new guests, the three young women turned to the door and when Laura recognized Werner among them, they froze. Immediately she felt a tingling sensation in her abdomen, in her head she heard the words he had said to her and she noticed how her pussy got a little wet. It made her uncomfortable, the blood shot down her cheeks and fearful that Werner might discover her and come over, or that her friends might notice something, she started, somewhat confused, a new conversation.

Werner had seen Laura sitting at her table immediately, but for the moment he preferred to ignore her and make her believe that he hadn't noticed her. He sat down with his friends at the bar and only occasionally stole a glance at the three young women.

After the first beer, however, he got up and went straight to the table of the three, sat down with them unasked as last time and introduced himself to the other two women. He talked to them animatedly for a few minutes and then politely asked them to join him and his friends at the bar. Laura was not at all happy, but Anja  and Julia agreed, so they took their drinks and followed Werner to the bar. The men offered their bar stools to the young women and then introduced themselves in a friendly manner. They talked about everything. After a while the waitress joined them and they had a pleasant conversation.

As they talked, the bar emptied until they were the last guests that evening.

After a while the conversation subsided and in this silence Werner says: "Bring a round schnapps Johanna, then I'll show you something." Johanna, the waitress took seven glasses, filled them with schnapps and put them on the counter. Everyone took one, then they toasted themselves and emptied the glasses in one go.

"So, my dears," Werner continued, "now I'm going to show you something." "Laura get up!" Laura was surprised, but got up and stood in the middle of the round. "I want you to show us your nice plump tits." Silence, the men stared spellbound, shocked at Laura, Anja and Julia at Werner and Johanna watched the events from their place behind the counter. Anja was just about to be outraged when she saw Laura slowly pulling her t-shirt over her head, then opening her bra and standing there with her bare chest the next moment. Werner now went very close to her and whispered in her ear, "I bet it makes you horny too," Laura prayed. The other two women were uncomfortable with the situation and the two men were also unsure how to behave, only Johanna watched everything intently. Anja and Julia asked Laura to get dressed and go again, but Werner instructed her to stay seated and be calm in a harsh tone.

"Now slowly brush your pants and panties down." Laura was disgusted to be treated like this in front of her friends and these strangers, but instead of contradicting, she slowly brushed down her pants. The pants gathered over her shoes. "Take off completely," said Werner and then added, without taking her eyes off her, "please help Anja." Anja was amazed, but as if remotely controlled, she got up and helped her friend pull her pants over her shoes. As she knelt in front of her naked friend she noticed how very slowly the excitement rose in her.

"But that's really enough now!" Julia brought out. "Well, if Laura thinks it's enough, she can say it at any time." Laura remained silent, wanting to say something, but couldn't utter a word. Now Werner took another step towards her, took her by the waist and began to circle her in the middle of the audience. Everyone was staring at the young woman in the middle, watching her beautiful body with excitement. After a few turns, he put her face to the counter so that she was between Anja and Julia and could look Johanna in the eye. He instructed her to brace herself on the counter and take a step back. In this position, she stretched her firm butt straight in Werner's direction. He ran his hands over the inside of her thighs and effortlessly pressed them apart with gentle pressure. Laura now offered the group a great sight as she stood so naked with her legs spread in the middle.

"Ok, if our little Fickstute doesn't run out between her legs, we'll stop playing right away, but if she's soaking wet, we'll continue. Who looks? "Nobody moved." Well, the best thing is to test your sweet cunt yourself so that everyone knows how things are. Is that okay with you Laura? " Laura's decent side wanted to put an end to all this and one sentence would have been enough, but she couldn't utter a word. Instead, she noticed how her pussy was overflowing  and the next moment she felt the first finger between her thighs. A shiver ran through her and she moaned softly. "Soaking wet" she heard the man to her left say when he started fucking her cunt with his finger. After a short while he let go and she felt the other's hand. The latter penetrated deep into her column with two fingers, then pulled the fingers out again and then put three fingers back in again. The smacking sound could not be heard by anyone present.

"So now it's your turn girls" Werner said in the direction of the two young women. Anja reigned first, reached out and stroked her whole hand gently through her friend's dripping cunt. Laura groaned with pleasure and that seemed to drive Anja, she now penetrated deep into the hot column with several fingers and began to fuck her hand violently. As she let go, Werner looked closely at Julia. Julia did not move. "Go on now" Werner ruled and finally stretched her her hand out, briefly touched Laura's wet cunt and quickly pulled her hand back. She just nodded shyly, as a sign that she had felt Laura's lust.

"You don't like pussies, Julia?" Said Werner in a gentle but commanding tone. "Then come here and get my cock out." She didn't react, but the next moment the man next to her had also gently pulled her off the bar stool and pressed her to her knees in front of Werner. Now she seemed to have changed. Her tender hands opened her pants and pulled out Werner's semi-rigid cock. She had never seen such a big cock and couldn't hide her amazement. First she slowly started to play around the glans with her tongue, then she gradually worked on the whole beating until she let it slide into her throat as far as she could. The shy young woman who had been petrified on the bar stool a few minutes ago now seemed unable to get enough of this cock.

Werner had had enough of Julia's greedy mouth and finally wanted to penetrate the horny cunt standing in front of him. He now pushed Julia aside and put his acorn at the photo entrance of the young woman in front of him. With a strong thrust he penetrated completely into her, Laura groaned loudly and he remained there for a moment. Then he immediately began to fuck her with hard, quick punches. She groaned loudly, her knees trembling with every push and after a few seconds she screamed her first orgasm. Werner worked on her mercilessly.

Laura could hardly stand with lust anymore, so Werner pulled his cock out of her and now put her face to him on a bar stool. He was immediately deep in her again and rammed his spanking into her insatiable cunt again and again. She came again, screamed her next orgasm and a tremor ran through her whole body. With her, Werner also shot his load deep into her. After a few more bumps, he pulled his still stiff cock out of her and turned back to Julia. "Now lick my sperm and your friend's pussy juice from my cock, then maybe I will fuck you at some point."

Julia was just as greedy and horny as before about the shiny, wet cock.

Laura was still completely finished and sat on her bar stool, trembling and spreading her legs. From her fucked pussy her juice and Werner's sperm ran in streams onto the bar stool.

Johanna had come out from behind the bar.

"And you think you can stay out of Johanna?" Said Werner now in the direction of the bartender and winked at her "Clean her cunt, otherwise she'll mess up the whole facility." Johanna winked back, knelt on the floor in front of Laura and sipped the hot fuck juices that poured out of the freshly worked column.

"Well, that's it," said Werner when he had had enough of Julia's blowing arts. "I'm looking forward to next time Laura, and you two will also get to it, maybe the gentlemen will fuck you too, if they jerk off again afterwards can."

Werner left the shop.

Johanna continued to lick Laura's column for a while. Laura breathed deeply and moaned and wiedder quietly.

The other four watched the two of them and stroked themselves.

Then Johanna let Laura's cunt go and got up, leaned over to her ear and whispered, "Thank you, gas was good."

In a matter-of-fact tone, she said to the others that she had to cash in and close the shop.

The evening came to an end.

The End.

# *Friends plus*

A hot summer day. I jump under the cool shower to wash off the sweat of the long day. I'm looking forward to a nice evening, let myself be cooked by one of my best friends and already know that we will have a lot to talk about.

I know few men with whom I can talk about sex as openly as with Manuel. Most of the men I know are actually more prudish. In any case, with Manuel, I never take a leaf out of my mouth. The fact that I have never considered doing more with him is probably due to an unspoken agreement that we do not want to lose this beautiful friendship.

When I arrive, I can convince myself that his culinary skills actually do what he promised and, of course, the number one topic comes up in the first course and he tells me about his with shining eyes and a big grin on his face latest conquest. An affair that finally gives him what he needs: good, intense, loving sex without being in love and without obligation. I can understand him well. Too often an affair was over for me too quickly because the sex is not good or despite all freedom the unpleasant power games develop.

I am really happy for him and I am not surprised that he communicates his happiness quite specifically: "It was just so nice! For hours we smooched and fiddled like teenagers and I took my time. They thought it was as hot as I was then I put her between my legs for the first time - there is no more wet expression at all! I didn't even sleep with her, I licked her and did it with her hand and kissed her for hours. I tell you - that was so cool! There is simply nothing better than seeing a beautiful woman coming. " He shines with his blue eyes in somehow innocent joy and I am happy for him and for the woman. "She was blown away. Honestly: I think she still had good sex! It is so cool to get a woman to

I get a little jealous of the unknown, because Manuel really stands out from some other men who often don't give themselves and the woman time to slowly build up the tension. I think about it a little and inevitably pictures appear in my mind's eye: Manuel licking,  kissing, happily watching a groaning, writhing woman ... I get even hotter than it is in the small kitchen and it tingles between my legs.

After dinner, we lie on the couch and do what only friends can do together: trash TV and a few episodes of Enterprise afterwards. With a grin, he repeatedly assures me that my love of science fiction in his eyes makes me so sexy that I can't even imagine it. That's right, I'm happy about the nice compliment, but I can't take it very seriously. But hanging out together is somehow different today. Manuel moves closer to me than usual and his looks have changed.

They slide along my legs again and again and get stuck on my cleavage. I know that he likes how I look and how I dress and in fact I move more sensually than usual in the light skirt and the tight T-shirt. His looks do the rest and I literally bask in them.

At some point it becomes clear to me that he lets me decide whether we should keep the previously observed border or cross it and become "friends + ...".

No problem. I only think about what feels like 2 hours if we can get a "part time lovers, full time friends" thing. During this time, his presence feels better and better, and finally I gather my courage, snuggle up on his arm and after a few minutes we kiss.

His lips are soft and the kiss is what I call perfect: sensual and enjoyable, lips and tongues play with each other, during the kiss breaks we smile at each other and his bright eyes tell me: Hello, nice to see you!

We slide into a better position on the couch and press each other. Even though we've talked about sex so many times, I have no idea what's going to happen today.

From my lips he continues to kiss his neck, neck, ear and moan softly and gently. "You just smell too good!" The summer, the sultry heat and the excitement mix in my fragrance and it makes me totally hot to see what desire it triggers in him. I offer him the places where the body scent collects: I lift my hair so that he can kiss me on the neck, the elbow, the lower back. He licks and kisses me there with increasing wildness and lets his hands slide under my skirt. I feel how wet I am. I know how he likes it when a woman flows beneath him, and yet I still can't let him go to my column. I need a little more, I have to greet him even better before I can let him on my pussy.

And we take the time to kiss each other for minutes, to whisper loving words, our hands play with each other. We both have a big, happy smile on our faces.

After a tender eternity, our kisses become more passionate again and his touch firmer. I feel the pleasure running through my whole body and my legs open by themselves. How I enjoy it when my body takes over the directing! Manuel's patience is rewarded and he takes off my last clothes. I lie naked in front of him and his eyes give me countless compliments. He kisses all over my upper body between my legs. My fingers open my vulva and I can feel his hot breath and his soft warm tongue. He groans and buries himself in my damp, warm, fragrant pleasure center. His tongue finds my clitoris and caresses it with quick movements. "Slower!" I ask him and he willingly accepts my wish. I moan when his tongue slowly and tenderly strokes my swollen, sensitive flesh. I forget the time and until only soft, warm, moist, cool.

When he kisses me, I taste myself and it makes me hornier. He continues to lick and keeps pushing his tongue into my narrow opening. I want to feel it deeper and pull it up to me. His fingers slide into my column and he finally penetrates me. He unerringly heads for my G-spot and this horny, firm inner massage gives me a kick that I can hardly describe. One finger quickly runs out of me and moans loudly as he adds another. I find a rhythm and he picks it up, fucks me with his fingers and carries me to orgasm through the precise massage. I tremble and moan and the knowledge that he now has the greatest pleasure in me, my pleasure a thousandfold.

Break. Drinking water. Talk. Laugh. Kiss.

And further: my soft, open and pulsating cunt picks up his cock and I enjoy the slow sliding in. I greet him in me, feel exactly how big it is, how firm it feels and feel it with the muscles in my vagina. I fit in perfectly. I smile happily at Manuel and pull him all the way into me. He groans and begins to push himself into me. At first he holds back, but I want his passion, I silently ask him to take me. I trust him give my body to him. I moan as he increases his pace and go with him, increase the movements of my pelvis, press against him and open my legs as much as possible. We enjoy the deep, passionate fuck and my pussy and his cock celebrate a horny, lusty party.

Again and again he takes a short break, cools down to extend the game, then shoves his cock deep into my waiting, open cunt, kisses me and lets me heat him up again.

We fuck ourselves up and his eyes change. "I'm coming. Okay?" The fact that he asks actually makes the answer superfluous for me: he doesn't just want to squirt in me, he wants the perfect moment for it. "Yes! Come on!" He smiles, his face relaxes again,

I can feel his cock even more present in me and I ride with him on his wave. I feel with him how his cock starts to twitch, how every thrust gets  even more intense, I moan with him and enjoy his orgasm as he meant before.

Then we smile happily and I know that I have found one of the rare "friends + ..." with him.

The End.

# *Then we are already two*

I live with my mother (47) in a small house on the outskirts of our home village, my father died in an accident about ten years ago.

We have always had a very intimate relationship and actually talk about everything (she knows that I am no longer a virgin and I know from her that she has no boyfriend but a dildo to relax, as we said we talk about everything) in my life No girlfriend at the moment, we broke up three months ago.

So much for the two of us

It's Friday evening my mother went out with her best friend, I stayed at home in front of the telly.

It is just before twelve o'clock when my mother comes home, I am sitting on the couch in the living room because the TV is connected to the Internet and I can stream films here.

Mom comes into the living room she has a blouse and a nice tight mini on which her beautiful long legs (she is barely 1.80 tall, has beautiful but not very big breasts, a B cup and a well-shaped butt) shows off, she arrives from behind the couch, I greet you with "hey mam how was it?"

She hugs me from behind and gives me a kiss on the cheek and says it was funny.

I smell the alcohol in her breath, she squeezes me again and then comes around the couch and sits next to me.

What are you looking at? "Ne comedy" I say to her.

Can I watch?

Sure mom, just started.

The film runs approx. 20 min. Mom grabs a pillow and lays her head in my lap (she often does that so I don't think about it) I stroke her head she has fashionable short hair.

"mhhhh" that's nice she says

your blouse which is unbuttoned at the top and allows me to look through her lying position on her left breast, which is no longer completely covered by her lace-decorated bra. I can even see her nipple standing slightly.

I actually had no sexual thoughts about my mother so far, of course I had a look at her strings (she probably likes to wear them) and her bras when they were hung up to dry after washing.

The sight of her breast naturally made my cock slowly become stiff. I just hope she doesn't notice any of it (I only have a shirt and a boxer shorts because it's summer and quite warm), luckily there is  a pillow between her head and my cock.

So I continue to stroke her head and enjoy the view of her breast.

Slowly it gets a little uncomfortable in my step so I move my pelvis a little, Mam lifts her head to look at me and asks "Is everything okay?"

Yes, it was just a bit uncomfortable. I probably get a slightly red face.

Mam notices and asks again if something is and why am I blushing?

I decided to tell her the truth that I got stiff from looking at her chest (as I said we are talking about everything)

she looks at me, then down at herself and starts to smile "I'm sorry. I didn't know that I lie there so frankly ".

"No problem mom" I say to her.

She looks at me for a long time and then says "thank you for always being so open to me, I love you my darling"

but you are always honest with me, I say.

That's true.

The next question from her surprises me.

"May I see your cock?" She asks.

Now I'm flabbergasted how does she figure it ???

You know what he looks like after all I'm your son.

"Yes, of course, but that was a while ago when I last saw you naked".

You saw my breast too, she winked at me.

But that was a coincidence and I'm sorry I didn't say anything!

"Hey, it's fine!" She says, looking at me strangely.

Mam starts to unbutton her blouse and takes it off.

My mouth is completely dry, I watch my mother reach behind her and open her bra and pull him forward.

With bare breasts she looks at me and says "now it's no accident"!

I don't know what to say and stare at my mother's breasts.

Do you like my tits? she asks me.

I can only nod.

May I see your cock now? Is your next question.

I take the pillow from my crotch up my butt by myself and pull my boxers down, through her bare breasts and the horny situation my dick is still rock hard.

"Mhhhh you have a nice cock she says and bites her lip slightly.

I stammer a" thank you "and ask her why she actually wanted to see him?

She says that she hasn't seen a real cock for a long time, just a dick Seeing plastic is not the same as a real pulsating cock.

Mom comes close to mine with her face and says "Thank you"

I ask her for what? (I know stupid question)

She answers "for your openness"

And that you show it to me!

And for the compliment that you give me that you get stiff at the sight of your old mother, she smiles at me.

You are not old and who does not get a hard look at the sight must be blind.

She is still smiling at me.

Then she kisses me on the mouth, only very timidly then more and more stormily I get involved and join in.

I feel her tongue on my lips and also insert my tongue, we smooch like freshly in love, she sucks on my tongue which makes me incredibly horny.

Without thinking about it, I start to knead her breasts and play on her nipples, mom moans in my mouth and I feel her fingers play on my dick.

She stops our smooching and looks at me full of lust.

"Do you want to continue?" Comes her question.

I look into her face and ask

"and you?"

She comes to my ear and says I'm just so horny for you and your tight cock that I just don't care that we are mother and son!

I kiss her and tell her that it only makes me hornier!

"Then we are already two!" She says and presses my face against her tits.

Immediately I grab one of your hard nipples and suck it into my mouth, my mother moans loudly and begins to work my cock with my hand, which makes me groan with her nipple in my mouth.

Mam takes my head in her hands and looks at me

She tells me to close my eyes and lean back!

I am a little disappointed that I can no longer take care of her breasts, but do as I please, lean back and close my eyes.

My mother pulls my shirt over my head and gives me a passionate kiss on the tongue, I feel her kissing my body down when she arrives in my crotch, she takes off my boxers completely and stays on the floor in front of me.

I feel her hot breath on my glans the next moment "my head explodes" my mother's tongue licks and sucks on my balls, I start to moan and say "oh my god you're driving me crazy mom"

She kisses and licks my shaft along the direction of my plump acorn and pulls my foreskin all the way back, she plays with her tongue on the ribbon below my acorn.

Then it is as far as she licks my glans I feel her warm wet mouth that sucks my cock.

I moan "you're so horny"

I can't stand it anymore and open my eyes and see my mother as she has my cock in her mouth and looks at me.

She sees that I am looking at her, lets my stiff slide out of her mouth and says "well, you shouldn't be looking"

I'm sorry, Mom didn't see how you blow my dick I couldn't take it anymore.

"then enjoy the show," she says, smiling at me knowingly.

My mother takes my hands and puts them on the back of her head, then she opens her mouth and only picks up my acorn, she looks me in the eyes expectantly.

I understand what she wants and rather lower her head her horny lollipop deeper, I feel like more and more of my cock finds place in her mouth and moan again. Only when I feel the tip of my nose on my belly do I pull her head with my fingers back up in her hair.

We repeat the hot game very slowly and with relish. Five minutes later I speed up the action.

Saliva and moan comes out of my mother's mouth as I fuck her in the mouth. Another five minutes later I notice that I will not be able to hold out much longer and will soon cumshot.

I also tell my mother.

She lets my cock slide out of her mouth and smiles at me and says "I know my darling, the twitching has already betrayed you" she winks at me and takes my cock back in my mouth and starts fast and hard on me suck.

Less than two minutes later it comes out of me, since Mam only has my acorn in her mouth, she can easily collect everything in the mouth that I 'give' her, I hear how she swallows everything and continues to suck on my acorn until nothing comes and my cock in her mouth is slowly getting smaller.

I take her face in my hands and pull her up to kiss me. I don't care that her mouth tastes of my 'juice'.

Then I tell her that I love her.

She looks at me and says that she also loves me and kisses me again.

She has my cock back in her hand and scratches my testicles,

I her breasts again.

My mother looks at me and asks me "do you want to lick my pussy darling?"

She seems to read my answer in my eyes, stands up and turns and pulls her mini down over her hot buttocks, bending down and presenting me with her thong, I can see the thin piece of fabric getting lost between her beautiful buttocks.

My heads go in the direction of these beautiful curves, I kiss their rear

suction their fragrance, my mother groans.

She leans forward, I grab her string on the right and left and pull down while I spread more and more kisses on her cheeks.

Mam gets out of her string, takes a step forward and turns to me.

My gaze is on her partially shaved pussy, her labia are slightly sticking out, her clitoris is laughing at me.

Mom looks at me and says "do you still want to taste my pussy?"

"I just don't want anything more than that!" I say.

She says "come with us, we go to my bedroom! There is more space for the two of us in bed".

I follow Mam to her bedroom.

She lies down in her bed, spreads her legs and says "then come and lick your mom's horny column!"

I won't let that be said twice, and I go to my mam's bed with my tail bobbing.

I support myself to the left and right of her body and search for hers with my lips.

We start a wild smooching, in the course of this I kiss my lips towards her middle body, caress her breasts, work her nipples very gently with my teeth.

With my mother's moan in my ears, I kiss further towards her belly button and further towards her pussy.

Arrived at the goal I start my game and lick several times through its complete gap, stop at the clitoris and work on this sensitive area for a minute or two.

When I feel hands on my head that ask me to continue.

I see my mother's eaten face, which is writhing with closed eyes and groaning.

My mind shoots' what are you doing? You lick the horny column of your own mother and just can't imagine anything better than this moment! '

Still listening to my thoughts, I hear my mother say that I should turn because she wants to suck my cock.

Nothing better than that! No sooner said than done, I'm not really under her because she already has my cock in my mouth and I have her snatch in front of my face.

How addictively I lick it off again.

The End.

# *Bea*

I really experienced it exactly the same way and wrote nothing about it.

*

We met on the Internet. What struck me immediately about her were her sky-blue, clear, intense eyes, her sensual, full lips and her black hair. An angelic face and her eyes looked with the innocence of a newborn, blue-eyed angel baby.

The first time we saw each other was at the tram station near her apartment. Then we drove to me. We were still very reserved, almost like teenagers, but we were grown-ups. The first kiss, like that of two post-adolescents, brought our upper bodies closer together, while our legs didn't move an inch towards each other.

She was very sensual, knew exactly what she wanted. I noticed that at the first meetings. She gently pushed my hands back when I stroked too close to her breasts. The touch of her lips was like revelations, electric shocks, which sent thousands of signals through my body and made my mind release hormones in abundance.

She noticed that her touches made me react so intensely and she didn't just make fun once of her tender bites in my throat, or even in my arms.

When we first slept together, it was a struggle between our lust. "I want to sleep with you now," she said, pulling me into my bed. We didn't bother to delicately explore our erogenous zones. No, we fell over each other, pulled our clothes off our bodies, and all we had to do was aim as quickly, deeply and intensely as possible. My member  was immediately available hard and stiff and stormed her vertical smile like the hordes of a Ginghis Khan. I fucked her wildly, almost brutally, deeply, snorting, moaning her wet vulva gave her intense feelings when my shaft rubbed against the tight muscle of her vagina. She came several times, screamed, cried, moaned and encouraged me to fuck her even faster and deeper, wrapped her leg around me and spurred a horse on with her heels, setting the pace for me. Steaming with lust, sweating and panting, I hammered my cock into her again and again until I sprayed my sperm deep into her.

She could turn her lust on and off like a light and used her body to piss me off. One morning, shortly after getting up, she was standing in the kitchen, wearing a sweatshirt and a thong. When she noticed that I was coming into the kitchen, she held out her butt to me like a bonobu in heat. The morning latte that was just fading away changed my mind and unfolded to its full splendor. I stood behind her and let her feel how much part of my body wanted her. She pressed her butt against my swollen limb, shook it into the crack between her buttocks, and began to irritate it even more with gentle, circular movements of her lower abdomen. All too readily, she let me put the thin thread of her thong aside,

She seemed to like such spontaneous fucks. Because less than half an hour after our quickie in the kitchen, she lay down without a word on the cleared breakfast table and signaled to me that she wanted more, which I was only too happy to give her.

We actually wanted to watch a little TV. We sat side by side on the couch, as good as teenagers. I don't remember how it started, but I think I accidentally nudged her while she reached for her glass. Immediately she pounded me tenderly, whereupon I moaned very theatrically with pain. This in turn incited her and she pinched my arm. Again I complained my pain exaggeratedly. We laughed. I gently pushed my index finger into her ribs, she squealed as she winced at the unexpected touch. She took my forearm and bit it lightly. This time I wasn't moaning with pain, but a thousand small needles seemed to pierce my skin, hit my receptors and spark a thunderstorm of pleasure. She looked at me and I saw in her eyes what she was going to do:

I was only too happy to let her take turns scratching and biting me. I felt her touch in an intensity I had never known before. Again and again I fended off her attacks, but only to the extent that she didn't stop there, but was repeatedly spurred on by my moaning.

She no longer concentrated only on my arms, but extended her tender biting on my neck, stroking my chest or holding on to my hips. She was sitting on me more now than on the sofa. I enjoyed the touch of her soft, full lips and moaned lustily whenever I felt them on my skin, followed by my pointed teeth.

She had pushed my shirt up, her hands hooked on my waistband, and her mouth approached my left breast. All of my muscles stiffened in anticipation of the next emotional chaos, which regularly followed their tender attacks. Her head shot forward like a bird, her teeth encircled my nipple, I reared up because I was expecting the pain, Instead, the teeth fell back, her lips wrapped around the stiff protruding wart, her tongue flicked out and flicked over them around.

My moaning said more than my cock, which she was sure to burst, which she definitely felt on her thigh. She let go of my chest and looked deep into my eyes. Her eyes were mesmerizing as she slid between my legs, her hands still hooked into my waistband. Slowly, her hands slipped from both sides towards the button that she slowly opened. Her eyes were still looking at me intensely, anticipating and observing. With a sliding movement she held the waistband with one hand while the other slowly pulled the zipper down. Hypnotized by her look and my lust, I lifted my pelvis a little and she brushed down my pants and shorts.

She was still looking at me with her not so innocent, but still deep blue eyes. Between my eyes stood my limb, erect, ready, smooth and throbbing. She gently stroked the foreskin down, increased the pressure a little, and pushed her hand down further until the glans puffed up a little more.

They had never blown me before. We always had our hot, almost brutal sex, which only concentrated on our genitals. How many times had I imagined that these lips could one day close around my glans, causing her feelings that I was unable to imagine.

She seemed to have guessed my dreams. She was still looking at me, a devil with angel eyes, but now lowered her eyes and looked at my stiff cock. Her full, voluptuous lips slowly approached my cock. She tenderly breathed a first kiss on my acorn. A firework of emotions exploded in me. The rockets shot higher and higher as she also slid her tongue down the bottom of my shaft, turned around on the scrotum and flicked again to the tip. Then her red lips encircled the entire glans for the first time. In slow motion, no much slower, they continued to slide down, stopped briefly at the acorn wreath and then cost the body. My acorn tapped briefly on her palate and, as if there was a switch, her mouth moved back again. Did she know what feelings did it spark in me? No, this orgammus did not come with giant strides, I was just about to do it, and her lips formed the obstacle that blocked it and at the same time attracted it. Again and again her lips slid over my totally sensitive, irritated and ready to inject cock, but still did not allow orgasm. Her hands were almost motionless on my hips as she gently sucked.

Again she looked into my eyes. I almost didn't notice it because I had my eyes half closed and rolled. A light breath of air on my acorn signaled that her lips had left her free. At the same time, I felt the gentle tingling of her tongue on my shaft. She licked the acorn wreath, kissed it, and traced the furrow between the shaft and the glans with the tip of her tongue. When she reached the ribbon, her lips shot together with her tongue in a tender, smacking kiss, which she repeated after a quick look at my acorn.

My God, how I would have loved to spray now! Everything in me was ready to storm the summit, but I was still waiting for the final command from her lips.

Should I let her know? Nothing is worse than when a woman pulls her mouth out in the middle of an orgasm because she doesn't want to have cum in her mouth.

Would she hold out until I finished spraying? Or would she back down? The thoughts swirled in my head, could not sort themselves out because only my instinct prevailed.

Fuck it, I would just let it come. If she then withdraws, then it was at least the damn hottest blowjob.

Again and again she covered my cock with small, lustful kisses like only women who find it fun to spoil a man. Her right hand now encircled the root of my shaft and pulled the skin all the way down.  At the same time, she pushed her lips back over my glans, only sucked on it lightly and started to put her mouth all over my cock and then slowly pull it back.

Actually, I thought that the feeling that I had seemed to feel for ages could not be topped. It wasn't a storm to orgasm, but an incredibly intense approach. Again and again her lips rubbed against my glans, sucked on the shaft. I kept thinking "Now!" and again and again I stayed a little bit, put more pressure behind my prostate. My moaning now filled the room permanently, paired with her light puffing and moaning. The orgasm crept up very slowly, seemed to approach on the back of intense feelings and announced itself more and more intensely. The sweet pain, the pressure on my prostate, was immeasurable. Her lips sucked lightly on my glans, her tongue rubbed the bottom of my cock and made me delight,

As slowly and intensely as he had announced, he came vehemently and impetuously.

When Bea noticed that I was ready, she pushed her lips even more intensely over my glans, sucked in my shaft and let her tongue dance on the ribbon.

With a primal scream, the first fountain of my sperm shot deep into her throat. She didn't flinch! I roared with lust when more splashes left my cock and flooded her mouth. In my exploding feelings and in the chaos of the hormones, I felt her swallow my juice. Only when there was really not a drop left did she let go of my cock, which was always stiff.

Now I saw her face contorted with lust. "I want to come too" she groaned and sat on my cock, rubbing her vulva through the jeans on him. This touch seemed like an electric shock to her, the switch flipped in a split second and she groaned her orgasm Wildly twitching and trembling wildly, her orgamsus shook her through and drove her wet lust through her pants in no time.

We lay on top of each other, her head on my shoulder, completely unable to move and slowly realized what our lust with us had started.

Our relationship didn't even survive the early days. Out of a stupid argument, she left my apartment one night and did not answer for two days. When she was finally ready to talk to me again, I was too stubborn.

But this experience, in the intensity of lust and feelings, I will never forget.

The End.

# *Our dream couple*

An unexpected bi foursome.

As our readers already know, our stories are always based on real events. This is also the case with the following description.

As was often the case in the past, we published our search for a bi-pair in a well-known contact magazine and received around 20 letters. However, only three couples came into question, as they did not live too far away and we also liked the enclosed photos. So we formulated our reply letters and gave our telephone number so that you could talk in advance and then make an appointment for a first meeting. We had the first call just three days later and the other two calls the following day. All calls were very positive and sometimes even very hot. Now we were spoiled for choice and decided to meet all three couples once without obligation in order to be able to make a selection in this way.

We were in our late 30s and early 40s and the first couple invited us to their private home. Both were older than us and we sat down in their living room. He was a rather unassuming slim man and she was an attractive resolute woman. We first talked about everyday things and later came up with our respective sexual ideas. We sat next to each other on a sofa, while our hosts sat in an armchair on either side of us. During the conversation, the woman began to loll around in the armchair, so that we could clearly see that she was not wearing panties under her skirt. She was wearing black stockings and angled her legs so that we couldn't miss her dark hairy pussy. Every move she made was very affected,

We met the second couple in a restaurant. They were about our age and the mood was very relaxed. Spontaneously they invited us to their apartment and arranged it so that he sat next to Beate and she next to me. Then they showed us videos on which they could be seen on the nudist beach and later on having sex with another couple. During the demonstration she snuggled up to me and he  began to stroke Beate's breasts. I thought I saw that

Beate wasn't feeling well when his hands went under her sweater and stroked her bare breasts. For this reason, I stayed idle at first and waited. He went on steadfastly, trying to slide a hand in Beates jeans while his wife asked me to help her open a bottle of wine in the kitchen. Arrived in the kitchen

Of course, it all made me horny, especially since she stroked the bump I had and was about to open my pants. I made her understand that we don't like sex in separate rooms and pulled her back into the living room with me. It was then immediately clear that Beate did not want sex because she was still sitting cross-legged idly while he had pushed up her sweater and sucked on the nipples. Apparently he hadn't been able to reach Beates's column from the front, but the jeans were open and his hand was deep in the back of the pants, so he probably had access that way. Back on the sofa, his wife pushed her skirt up and spread her legs. Again she took my hand and led it to the swollen clit. Then she opened the zipper of my pants, shoved her hand in and rubbed my bare cock. Apparently she was extremely horny, because after a short time she suddenly got up, went to Beate and tried to open her legs and take off her jeans.

Beate reacted immediately by literally jumping up and freeing herself from his grasp. Then she closed her jeans, pushed the sweater back down and said that she just wanted to meet and not want sex. It then only took a few minutes for us to leave the apartment. Later in the car, she told me that he smelled strongly of sweat, so that the desire had passed. So we already had two unsuccessful attempts and were already afraid that the third attempt might end up like this.

The third couple was significantly younger than us and we had invited them to our home. They were there on time and even brought a gift in the form of a bottle of champagne. Both were fairly unremarkable people, he was blonde and she was dark-haired. As is always the case at a first meeting, you first assess each other before an open and easy conversation is possible. So we sat in our living room and talked about God and the world. Beate and I often made eye contact and it soon became clear that we both liked this couple. Obviously, this was based on reciprocity, because the mood eased very quickly. Tina and Rolf, as they were called, then very openly expressed their positive opinion of us and suggested drinking brotherhood. We gladly agreed to this suggestion and started with the usual procedure. It was funny that after I just wanted to shake hands with Rolf, Tina demanded the obligatory kiss of both men and women. I'm absolutely bi, but I've never kissed a man on the mouth. Of course it was not a problem, but I had to register again that women are much more open about it.

We sat down again and went on to the comfortable part. The topics became increasingly intimate and we shared each other's experiences and preferences. Beate and I had actually assumed that this meeting, like the other couples before, would only serve to get to know each other without any commitment. However, the very detailed experience reports led to a very horny atmosphere, which apparently captivated us all and led to the name of more and more details. For my part, I was extremely horny and Beate showed the first reddish spots on her neck, which she always got when she got hot.

Again it was Tina who surprised us with her openness by suddenly saying that she would burst with lust if she didn't get sex now. Then she suggested that we all go to the bedroom to get to know each other better. It was like a salvation and we all immediately got up and went to the bedroom. Once there, everyone stripped down to their underwear and lay down on the bed. As a matter of course everyone stroked everyone without touching the intimate zones. This time it was Beate who found that the men's briefs had mutated into tents and that there had been leaks in the women. With these words, she began to examine Rolf's tent more closely. She knelt down next to his legs, felt the huge bulge, briefly jerked the hard stick with the panties and then released him from his prison. Since Beate knelt so provocatively and stretched her butt up, Tina took this opportunity to stroke one hand gently over her butt and thighs and then to let her hand disappear under the fabric on the side of the leg.

Beate twitched at these touches and let her pelvis rotate slightly. This, however, without letting go of Rolf's plump cock, which she was working on with her mouth. Tina was lying diagonally next to Beate, so I had to kneel on the floor to reach her. I did this too, watched her make smacking noises between Beate's legs with my hand and devoted myself first to her large breasts for such a slim woman. I quickly removed the disturbing bra and sucked on the stiff nipples while she slid directly into my panties with my free hand. There she pushed my foreskin far back, spread the first few drops of joy on my glans and then put her fingers in her mouth and licked it off. She did the same with her fingers, that she had previously sunk in Beate's column. I was now licking my way down her body, first sucking in the scent of her shame and without hesitation took off her rather wet panties. A wonderful cunt came to light, the dark hair  was trimmed short. It was amazing for me because there was a wet open column in front of me that had absolutely all the attributes that I love so much. By this I mean an above-average pronounced venus mound, a pea-sized clit, slightly protruding inner lips and last but not least the well-groomed trimmed hair. whose dark hair was cut short. It was amazing for me because there was a wet open column in front of me that had absolutely all the attributes that I love so much. By this I mean an above-average pronounced venus mound, a pea-sized clit, slightly protruding inner lips and last but not least the well-groomed trimmed hair. whose dark hair was cut short. It was amazing for me because there was a wet open column in front of me that had absolutely all the attributes that I love so much. By this I mean an above-average pronounced venus mound, a pea-sized clit, slightly protruding inner lips and last but not least the well-groomed trimmed hair.

After I first enjoyed the hot fragrance typical of women and licked the escaping juice, I rubbed the clitoris with two fingers until the clitoris peeped out of its hiding place in the skin fold. Then I wrapped my lips around it and worked it with my tongue so that Tina reared up and moaned loudly. When I then carefully felt a finger in the heavily oozing opening and quickly reached her G-spot, her upper body shot up so that she was more likely to sit on the bed. Her eyes and mouth were closed and she held her breath. Seconds later she blew out the jammed air and sank back into the lying position with her lower body twitching. I had forgotten everything in the whole process around me and only now realized that Tina had obviously pulled down my panties and enclosed my plump cock with a firm grip. I had also missed the fact that Rolf had been lying supine under Beate and also buried his head between her legs. Beate continued to suck on his crossbar.

Tina, who had recovered quickly, now turned to the side, took my cock, which was tense to burst, in her hand, pulled her foreskin far back, licked the glans with relish, and then put her mouth over the shaft so far that I was in toasted her throat. While alternately sucking and licking, she gently stroked my balls and pressed my rosette with a fingertip. I continued to kneel next to the bed, alternately stroking her breasts and pussy, and at the same time I was able to watch Rolf undress my Beate and suck at her crevice like a thirsty thirst. All of this led to the tingling sensation that announced the orgasm that was developing. I was just horny and prepared to inject my juice deep into Tina's throat. However, this did not happen because Tina had apparently noticed my orgasm coming up. She squeezed my eggs vigorously, let go of me and went to Beate, over whose back she leaned and grabbed her breasts and pussy with both hands. Rolf, who was disturbed by his action, crawled out from Beate, a little puzzled. I could see that he was also about to be discharged because his face was very red and his tail was pointing upwards.

I liked the sight and I didn't hesitate to take this tight part in my hand and jerk off lightly. While our women were licking each other in the 69 position, we men now had each other's cocks in our hands and jerked each other. Rolf's cock felt great and the lust rose in me again. I wanted more, so I lay down next to him so that each of us could reach the other's tail with his mouth. Rolf tenderly jerked my latte and licked my shaved sack while I licked the hot drops from his glans and then patched this hot cock with my mouth. It wasn't long before I suddenly felt this sweet taste in my mouth. Very weak at first, but then he sprayed violently, so that I could hardly keep up with the swallowing. It was so cool that my juices started to rise again. I surprised him with the first splash, because it slapped his forehead. Rolf hastily put his mouth over my glans and greedily swallowed the rest of my load.

We licked our tails for a while until they were completely sperm free and flaccid. Then we looked at our women, who continued to lick each other's columns and groaned loudly. It wouldn't be long before they had their orgasms too. We didn't want to bother her and were just about to get our drinks out of the living room when Beate reacted violently and with a wheezing breath to the tongue games of Tina. Of course, we were now eagerly waiting for Tina to have her orgasm too. However, this continued for a while and happened when Beate, after she had recovered, slowly put her hand into Tina's soaking wet cunt. Tina clutched Beate's wrist, leaned forward and roared her lust out. It was a damn awesome sight Seeing the wide open hole between her spread legs as Beate pulled her hand out and rubbed the wetness on Tina's breasts. Of course, we men couldn't keep our fingers with us and stroked our women for a while before we got the drinks.

Unspoken it was clear to all of us that this was not the end of this evening, so we made ourselves comfortable on the bed and recovered by caressing each other. It was just great that we understood each other so well, even though we had never met before. It passed about an hour in which we had got a little horny again with lively conversations. The mutual contact became more concrete, whereby it now amounted to the classic partner exchange. Rolf stroked Beate, who had her legs slightly bent and spread wide and I concentrated on Tina, who was half on me and licked my nipples. For a brief moment, I thought about inserting a porn DVD to fuel the mood. However, this was not necessary since we were all very busy again. Rolf knelt down next to Beate and pulled a cock ring over his upright cock while Beate scratched his sack. When the ring was in place, he gripped her cunt with one hand, which was still offered to him with her legs apart. I hadn't seen my wife in such a long time.

Tina continued to suck on my nipples so that I could barely reach her genitals. With a little effort I managed to reach between her buttocks with my arm straight and feel at least part of her cunt. Slowly she licked down on my body until she reached my cock. She knelt next to me and licked along my shaft to the eggs to my rosette, which she wetted with a lot of saliva. Then she swung over me so that her cunt was directly over my face, leaned back and began to slowly slide a finger into my back door. The smell of her column was overwhelming and I licked and sucked on it like a drowning one. Her finger in my intestine and of course the excitement of her increasingly wet cunt made my pleasure butt so hard that it hurt slightly. Tina groaned and jerked until she suddenly moved backwards, inserted my cock at lightning speed and rode me with quick and hard movements. She rested on my chest with both hands, twirling my nipples. In a very short time, her juice poured over my cock root and I only got her screams from afar, which she let out during her orgasm, as there was a loud rustling in my head as I pumped my sperm into her. She rested on my chest with both hands, twirling my nipples. In a very short time, her juice poured over my cock root and I only got her screams from afar, which she let out during her orgasm, as there was a loud rustling in my head as I pumped my sperm into her. She rested on my chest with both hands, twirling my nipples. In a very short time, her juice poured over my cock root and I only got her screams from afar, which she let out during her orgasm, as there was a loud rustling in my head as I pumped my sperm into her.

I stayed inside when she leaned forward and kissed me passionately. It was also loud next to us because Rolf fucked my Beate with hard bumps in the missionary position. With every bump it clapped loudly and Beate roared her lust out. I always loved to see her really enjoy sex with other partners, and this time it was. While my cock slackened from Tina's slippery cunt, I reached between Rolf's legs with one hand and squeezed his balls a little. I was just registering that everything was extremely wet there too, when he suddenly roared like a deer and discharged into my wife. I thought it was very cool and immediately grabbed his slippery cock when he pulled it out. I enjoyed sucking it clean and doing the same with Beate's cunt. The mixture of her juice and sperm is one of the hottest delights for me. Tina scurried into the bathroom and while I was crouching between my wife's legs, Rolf reached between my legs and gently massaged my cock. After everyone was in the bathroom one after the other, we went back to the living room because it was easier to sit there. Dressed only in underwear, we chatted until dawn and got along so well as if we had known each other for years. It was clear to all of us that we would spend many great hours together and made an appointment for the next weekend.

In fact, a very fulfilling time began with many very awesome experiences. We will report about it gradually.

The End.

# *Schoolgirl*

As always, it's about detailed sex, which shouldn't come as a surprise here. If you are offended by graphic, homo-erotic sex, bondage, dominance or spanking, please go somewhere else on the www. It shouldn't be that hard to find an alternative. Of course, all characters are fictitious, no real people have been harmed and everyone is much older than eighteen years. What else? All those who are not deterred have fun reading.

Schoolgirls

"Hey, are the magazines from deim Papa there? Shit, your old man is cooler than I thought. "

My best friend and I rummaged in her attic. Officially, because she's looking for some dress that might have ended up here someday. Unofficial because her father made us curious. The last time he cleared out a few weeks ago, he had been very vague and evasive about a few corners of the store.

Now I knelt in front of a box of porn magazines. But not any porn. These were first class bondage and fetish porn. High quality photos on glossy paper. Hardcore. When browsing, it quickly becomes apparent that Amanda's old man has a schoolgirl fetish. And the pictures of the naked, tied up and obscenely exposed, schoolgirl-trimmed porn beauties, who are forced to do all kinds of sex, drive me straight into my lap.

"Every man has a porn collection, so my dad is no exception. Look better what I found, "Amanda replies triumphantly.

I did her the favor and looked up.

" Maybe a porn collection, but not one. "

I forgot another version when I realized what I saw. Amanda was holding clothes. At first glance nothing was remarkable. On the other hand, I realized that the things were lacquer and leather, not fabric. And what she held in her right hand looked suspicious, like a school uniform like a Sailor Moon anime.

"Wow," it escaped me. My imagination clearly started to go through with me. In my mind's eye I saw myself first, then

Amanda, then again in tight, sexy fetish clothing. And a menacingly rising male shadow. It was certainly not a coincidence that he, even though I imagined me no details had to be Amanda's father.

"Wow. Yeah. Come on, we let the stuff even try. that could even fit."

the thought made a chill run down my back. when I mean When I wanted to moisten my lips with my tongue, I only noticed how dry my whole mouth was.

"No wonder," I amused myself, "all the moisture is needed further down."

The fact that I couldn't just touch and satisfy myself contributed to the build-up of lust, I found.

"Isn't that too risky? What if your old gentleman comes home earlier? "

" Oh what. If the Skat knocks, he never comes home before one. Mostly later. We still have hours. Apart from that, he meets a friend in Frankfurt today always so that he can drink. We don't have to  reckon with him before noon tomorrow. So let's not pinch. And please bring the box there. "

With these words and a second swing of clothes on her arms, she made her way to the stairs. After a last look at the porn collection, I grabbed the box it had pointed to. A large, bulky moving box that luckily wasn't too heavy. What was in there? Amanda must have looked inside. I speculated more fetish clothes.

In Amanda's room I dropped the box into a corner and joined her. We quickly sorted the costumes. A set of school uniform made of lacquer, already lying on the bed, obviously not suitable for school. A set made of leather and fabric that its wearer is likely to transform into an obscenely strictly dressed secretary. Or maybe a schoolmaster? A nun habit, a nurse costume, both made of lacquer, and a rather normal looking ball gown completed the small collection.

"I'll try this here. Why don't you take the school uniform? I bet you give a one a perverted school girl. You change in the bathroom, me here. But knock before you burst in here again. "

"Why? Are you afraid I'm going to get you naked? "I grinned. We'd seen each other so often, be it showering in the swimming pool or after exercising, or changing clothes when we spent the night together that it would have been silly each other to grace.

"no, but I bet the impression of clothes is sharper when you only see the end result. also, I bet you're already hot enough even to stare without my tits."

Shit, that was sitting. I couldn't think of a quick reply, so I preferred to shut up. She was right.

I silently picked up the school costume and headed for the bathroom.

"And no nonsense, yes. No dirty fumbling, and don't forget to wash your hands. "She had a really nasty grin on her face.

" Yes, mom, "I muttered defiantly as I slipped out of the room.

"I heard that, young lady."

"Yes, yes."

I had some fun in the bathroom. I couldn't resist pulling out. First I squeezed and caressed the breasts briefly. Then my fingers ran through the thick, black curls of my pubic and finally around the labia. However, I successfully resisted the temptation to penetrate myself.

The second fun was getting into the clothes. Everything was probably cut right from the start, but I still couldn't get rid of the feeling that the things were originally made for someone a little more delicate than me.

Hold-up, black stockings almost to the bar, a black thong that cut so deep in the crucial areas that it just felt cool and was almost invisible, a skirt that would be described as a mini, an exaggeration, a black push- up bra. The bra was awesome. Super tight lacquer he forced me to squeeze my breasts properly and squeeze until they finally rested satisfactorily in the shells.

The sight was almost obscene. The black varnish squeezed the white flesh up and up, causing my bust size to swell twice. At least visually. Something else was comfortable. But it felt great how the latex squeezed my breasts.

Above that, the white blouse, made of some stretch fabric. It seemed opaque, but of course the black bra was more than clearly visible below. The fact that the blouse was so tight over my body that it felt like a second skin didn't help the sight. Or just yet. It's all a matter of point of view. Or the objective. My nipples, now as hard as pebbles, wanted to drill holes in the material and were more than clearly visible despite the patent bra.

Where the top few buttons should normally have been, there was a yawning emptiness on this blouse. Only the button on the collar came back, underneath the fabric gaped in two semicircles. The neckline was so wide that the bra was clearly visible and my breasts were pressed into the opening. In addition a short, thick tie.

Finally I put my hair into two braids, one on the right and one on the left. The look in the mirror confirmed: I looked like the perverse caricature of a naughty schoolgirl. All that was missing were the fuck-me pumps and a lolly.

When I left the bathroom, I didn't know what I was looking forward to more: how Amanda would react to my costume or what she looked like.

Amanda was awesome. I hardly recognized her. Her long, red hair had been tied up in a strict bun, and the frame of a pair of glasses was enthroned on her nose. At the other end she was wearing black pumps, which she let easily rise over me, and an ankle-length skirt made of black leather. The seriousness of her ensemble was then broken by the blouse. She was wearing the same white sausage skin as I was. Only she was a little more rounded than me and both breasts and nipples were bigger. In one sentence, she stretched the stretch material to the limit. The whole thing looked somewhere between perverse and ridiculous. The black corset didn't help either, as it almost gave her a wasp waist and made her breasts look even bigger than they already were.

"Isn't that cool? It totally turns me on. How about you Gentlemen, that's a cutout, nothing is hidden from me. But it looks sharp. What do you

think of me ? " She spun around dramatically and I couldn't help giggling. Amanda, who had finished her turn, gave me a scathing look.

" So, young lady, do you find something amusing? you seen in the mirror? The young lady struts around like a cheap bitch, her tits half out of her blouse and her skirt short of decency. "Fuck me, boys," the whole wardrobe screams. "

It was terrifying how exactly she managed to mimic our principal's tone. She completely caught me on the wrong foot. Suddenly I became aware of how bitchy my outfit would really appear in everyday life. While her costume looked sexy and ridiculous, mine actually screamed 'fuck me'. With a few simple words in an imitated voice, she managed to put me on the defensive without any problems.

While I was still struggling for words like 'Hey, it was your idea to try the fetish stuff,' she grabbed my right hand, inspected the palm of my hand, and finally smelled my fingers. Which left me speechless even before I found the right words.

"And the young lady didn't wash her hands either. It is clearly cunt juice that I see and smell there. "

Now she has made it completely. In my mind's eye I actually saw Ms. Schroder standing in front of me and preaching a punishment. I  was intellectually certain that it was just happy But emotionally I felt completely caught and felt the heat shoot me in the face. I actually tried to apologize but only brought out incoherent stammering.

"Well at least the young lady was still decent, at least embarrassing But this stupidity, young lady, is absolutely unacceptable. It requires a more severe punishment than just a sermon. "

With these words, she jerked my hand so that I lost my balance and stumbled forward with a startled cry until I hit the bed frame. Before I knew it, Ms. Schroder / Amanda had tied my right wrist to the side of the bed with a leather cuff.

"Hey," I protested loudly, "this is no longer funny. Come on, let me go, Manda." I finally found my words again. It is about time. Otherwise I didn't fall for my mouth.

Instead of an answer, she gave me a hard pat on the butt. I cried out in shock.

"Tss, tss, young lady. You won't get away from me so easily this time. Anyone who behaves like a little bitch shouldn't be surprised if she is treated like a little bitch. "

My second wrist was encased in a leather cuff and tied to the bed. My girlfriend just ignored my complaining and ranting. It was dawn to me that the lack of physical resistance could easily be seen as consent and the verbal as part of our costume, and in fact I had to admit to myself that while part of me was startled, a little fearful, another part was still Which increased even more when Amanda began to stroke the skirt and the varnish nestled coolly against my skin.

"Come on, Manda, get rid of me. Slowly it's really not funny anymore. "

Instead of answering, she pushed the hem of the skirt up.

" Now, now, young lady. The punishment is well deserved, and nothing will stop me to carry it out. If the young lady said, If she wants to keep bothering my ears with her stupid whine, she'll have to get a gag, and what do we have here? Has the young lady still got some decency? Or did she speculate that such an inadequate piece of plastic would make the boys even sharper than a naked cunt? "

With these words, she grabbed the waistband of the lacquer panties and pulled roughly on it. I bit my lip to keep from moaning. It was rough, almost painful, but incredibly cool at the same time. I wanted to wiggle my butt to increase pressure and friction. But after my protests, I could hardly give in so quickly.

Then a loud clapping came to my ear, followed by a burning pain on my right buttock.

I cried out in surprise and slightly shocked and kicked out reflexively. I really didn't expect that.

"So so. The young lady is not only a bitch, she also gets pampy. We probably have to take other measures. "

She roughly tore the string down my legs, largely ignoring my shouting and beating. It took a little struggle, however, before she managed to tie my right, then my left ankle to the feet of the bed. When did she fix all of that? It all seemed so prepared, I suddenly noticed. Had she ever snooped around the attic and everything today was just a trap for me?

"So, young lady. I think we're almost ready now. If you present your ass so nicely, we can hardly ignore it. "

Clapping again and slight pain. Another cry of protest. That was choked off abruptly when she jerked my head up by the hair and stuffed the string between my teeth. The artificial taste of lacquer and that of my own excitement lay heavily on my tongue. I tried to push the part out of my mouth under an inarticulate curse, but she was too quick to wrap a piece of cloth tightly around my mouth and head. It didn't condemn me to silence, as I knew it from film, radio and television, but it dampened my protest. And probably more importantly, it made my protest completely incomprehensible.

"No wail, young lady, you wanted it that way. You will see, it is only for your own good. A bitch is only good to present her ass and get her cunt stuffed. That may be enough for a young lady like you, but at some point the ass becomes fat and wrinkled and the tits sag softly and apart from a few perverts, nobody likes to fuck such a thing. Therefore, young lady, you will have to learn this lesson. "

She emphasized every second word with a smacking slap on one or the other of the buttocks, and I just noticed what a lecture she thought I was. At first my riot and fidget was primarily a protest. But gradually the uncomfortable pain increased to real, burning pain. Accordingly, my screams became real cries of pain and my fidgeting to a vain attempt to escape the blows.

It took a few moments before I realized that the blows had stopped. My buttocks burned like fire and the edge of the bed frame painfully dug into my stomach.

Her hands coolly laid on my ass and gently stroked her cheeks. It felt really good and I had trouble suppressing a pleasant moan. Her fingers found the notch where they played over my anus for a  moment. I tried in vain to escape this unwelcome attention, although I had to admit that it felt good if I was honest.

Then she ran over the inside of my thighs.

"What do we have here? Looks like any educational measure is too late for the young lady. It's all soaking wet, and it's not sweat, wasn't it? "

She drove up to my column, and then two fingers stretched me out and made me shrug my hips. The groan that I involuntarily escaped sounded more like grunts in my own ears.

"The young lady can only grunt with lust. Maybe we should call her horny bitch instead. This cunt overflows like a blocked drain. "

The fingers in my vagina just felt cool. Much more intense than any masturbation, more intense than just about any sex I've ever had. As if the forced passivity increased feelings or my perception. I started to lose my rational thoughts, it felt too horny when she fingered me with my fingers, a third seemed to join the first two. I groaned my burning desire uncontrollably, wiggled and shrugged my hips so that the breasts danced wildly and the bed frame chased pain through my waist. Which gave my lust spice.

Oh god, I craved the climax as much as I wish these awesome feelings would never stop.

Four fingers.

Had my comments been understandable, Amanda would have heard me beg.

'Yes, don't stop. Keep it up. God, that's awesome. Further. Further. Oh god, please let me come. ' That or what, I thought.

"I was listening to you or I was going to go to my ears." Was what got to my ears.

Another finger. Another finger? I felt more spread than with a gynecologist, the pressure became almost unbearable. What the hell did Amanda do Did she try to put her whole hand in me? Then the tension eased when whatever had built up the pressure, jerked into me. I screamed in the gag as a small orgasm drove through my abdomen.

"Shit, I don't think so," I heard Amanda say in her own astonished voice. In her schoolmaster's voice, "The young lady doesn't seem to be just a little bitch. Rather a full-grown bitch. How many cocks are there? drove into this worn out cunt when a fist fits in there without problems? "

I could hardly believe what I was hearing. I actually had Amanda's whole hand in me. I would not have described the procedure as problem-free, but it felt cool anyway, and just the idea made me moan again.

I didn't know exactly what she was doing. The pressure in my vagina changed, sometimes it pressed more here, then there. The difference to a tail was not only the thickness, but above all the mobility. No tail in the world could rub me so well, in different places at the same time. Will I ever be able to fully enjoy normal sex again, I wondered?

And then my world sank to extremes as it clenched my hand into a fist and moved slowly back and forth, then faster and harder. Every time she hit my cervix, pain twitched through my abdomen, which paradoxically only made me hornier. Shrugging wildly and screaming in the gag, the last bit of reluctance was swept away when it came to me.

And it didn't stop. She kept hammering her fist into me and then started petting my clit. I screamed and screamed and screamed until I realized I was starting to hyperventilate. I don't think I lost consciousness. Not in the real sense anyway. But I was so lost in orgasm, pain and ultimately almost painful orgasm that I lost all sense of time and space. At first I couldn't get enough, and my fidget was the search for more. Then it got too much and the search for escape.

I have no idea when she stopped torturing me like this. Today she claims that I had shrugged easily for a quarter of an hour before I finally calmed down. In any case, I slowly emerged from my delirium. Which felt great. I felt light enough to create the illusion that I was floating and only the bondage kept me from climbing to the ceiling like a balloon. Euphoria flowed through me like a drug.

When my vision slowly normalized, the first thing I saw was a couple of bare feet. My eyes followed the long, slender legs of my friend, who was sitting in front of me with her bare abdomen. Her labia stared at me bald and damp shiny. The gag was gone.

"Ah, the young lady is receptive again. I have to admit that the performance was impressive and did not leave me completely unaffected. Therefore, young lady, it is now up to you to return the favor. "

She opened her thighs wider, which made me stare directly at the pink between the labia. I was still completely foggy, almost drunk with pleasure. Without thinking or hesitation I stuck out my tongue and reached out to reach her cute mouse. Totally unnecessarily Amanda grabbed my hair and pulled me towards her. At the same time she slid closer and finally I could reach her.

She hadn't left my performance untouched. Bugger me. Amanda was at least as wet as I was. And obviously not that far away. With an enthusiasm that I would have denied an hour ago, I started to lick it. Her taste was similar to mine, although it was less intense. Tart and sour, it filled my mouth. My tongues were accompanied only by heavy breath and occasional soft sighs. The hand in my hair alternated between rough tugging and tenderness.

I licked from her pearl to the anus, stuck my tongue as deep as possible into her juicy opening and nibbled and sucked on the small, sensitive skin flaps. Then I licked and pushed her again.

As expected, it wasn't long before Amanda came. Unlike me, it was quiet. Her occasional sighing stopped, only her breathing became harder. Her fingers clawed into my hair and dragged me deeper into her lap. My cry was smothered by her soft, hot flesh as her thighs closed around my neck.

She started screeching, more loud moans actually. Then she started to tremble. First the legs, then the abdomen and probably the rest of the body. I couldn't breathe between the tug on my hair and the pressure on her thighs, which made my efforts intensify. What would have been a big cock in my pussy horny.

She just didn't stop coming. There was hardly any change in her moaning, even though my ears were mostly filled with my own smacking and smelling. The tremors, on the other hand, became stronger and more uncontrolled, my whole body seemed to resonate in harmony. The sheet rubbing over my oversensitive nipples felt rougher and rougher. My hips twitched in anticipation.

Then she sighed and went limp. The legs slipped off my back and her fingers came out of my hair. Panting greedily, I sucked in the air, which found its way back to my lungs while muttering "Mmm, that was nice" and gently stroked my hair.

We stayed in this constellation for quite a while. I half enjoyed it, half quarreled with the fate that what brought Amanda satisfaction and relaxation had only rekindled my lust. A pleasure that I did not expect to be fulfilled today. How cool would be a real fuck now. Fuck single life.

Then the pain started to get really uncomfortable, especially in the shoulders and where the bed frame pierced my waist.

"Manda, seriously, can you please get rid of me? I really can not. "

She jumped, startled.

" Oh my God. Now, Tascha. I was so far away in Lala-land. I'm sorry. "

As she spoke, she crawled around on the bed and began to unfasten the straps. She babbled excuses and tenderness all the time, but I confess I was too distracted with my own thoughts to pay much attention to her.

That only changed again when she gently pulled me onto the bed and hugged me. Suddenly I had a big lump in my throat and had to fight the tears.

"It was so beautiful. Nice and incredibly cool. Thanks for that, Tasha. I hope I didn't go too far, "she whispered in my ear.

Still fighting with tears, I returned the hug and pressed myself close to her.

" It was totally awesome. A little extreme, but totally awesome. "

After these words I pressed my lips to hers and penetrated aggressively with my tongue. After a brief moment of resistance she gave in and our tongues started wildly. It felt like an eternity before our tongues and lips parted. Amanda was as breathless as I was.

"I have to confess this was the first time for me with a woman," Amanda whispered.

"Me too," I managed to say before I started to giggle uncontrollably. Amanda eyed me critically for a moment, then she started to giggle and a little later we were both shaken with laughter as we continued to hold each other and caress each other.

We gradually calmed down and slid into a more comfortable position. Amanda stuffed pillows into her back and leaned against the wall, I snuggled my back against her and enjoyed her tenderness.

"Do you think your old gentleman is still using this stuff?"

"Why? Did you make a fool of him?"

I felt the heat rise in my face. Good thing I was sitting with my back to her. I found her father really attractive and would certainly not mind having him tied up and fucked. Most recently, he had played a prominent role in my masturbation fantasies.

"No of course not. I mean, he might as well be my father, right? Age-related, and such. I'm just curious. "

" Yeah, sure. "

With these words she twisted my nipple so that I squealed in surprise.

"You have been keen on my old man for weeks. Or do you think I wouldn't have noticed you staring at him? You almost start drooling when you feel unobserved. "

" Ouch, don't do that, "I protested weakly, slapping her hand more symbolically. "You're just imagining it."

She twisted my nipple even more, her other hand slid up the inside of my thigh.

"Just admit it. There's nothing there. He did a good job for his age."

Her fingers reached my still soaking wet pussy. I squeaked and groaned, one hand around her wrist, the other behind her head.

"Oh god, keep going. Please go on. "

But after a short dance over my pearl, her fingers pulled back again. Her nails scratched my thighs. I twitched and bucked in search of the right contact. In vain. This beast.

" Still horny, mine Sweetie? No problem. I will send you on another flight. Just admit that you are keen on my dad. "

I was silent. Should she think what she wanted. What did it matter to her, whom I loved or who I was keen on. But I had made the calculation without the landlord. Or landlady, in that case.

She didn't stop teasing and torturing me and I was helpless to fight back. With moans and occasional squeaking when she pinched or scratched me somewhere, I squirmed in helpless excitement.

"You don't want to come? No problem, I'm having a lot of fun, I can go on like this for hours. "

And the sadistic bitch did that too. At least it felt like when I lost my sense of time for the second time in an afternoon. But then it was time, I couldn't anymore, I finally wanted to feel her fingers in my pussy, on my pearl, I finally wanted to COME.

"Damn, you perverted pig. YES, I want to BIRD your father. I want to feel his hard cock in my cunt. I want to COME, YES, I AM BANGED IN YOUR FATHER. Please let me come. Let me come. "

I screamed and sobbed almost hysterically. I still haven't understood why I didn't think to lend a hand and get myself over the crucial point.

" Well, go on just to you, this is his hard, stiff cock. Come for me. "

Even through my fogged mind, I heard the purr in her voice. And then I screamed my orgasm when she stuck two or three fingers in my pussy. In front of my eyes was her father, who rammed his cock into my hungry hole.

At some point I came back to Earth and still found myself with my back to Amanda in her arms, who caressed me gently, kissed and murmured tender nonsense. She gave me a few minutes of quiet rest. I felt so light and relaxed again and almost fell asleep.

"Mmm, fine," I muttered wearily.

"You know what? I think you should seduce my old man."

I was suddenly wide awake again. Was I right?

"What?"

"I mean , you better than such a bitchy cut that I don't even know. I also know when, and we practiced that a bit."

"Are you serious? You're trying to set me up with your father? "

"Why not? You have a crush on him and he certainly hasn't had sex since divorce. Unless he has any lovers or hookers on his business trips. I could also imagine a worse combination. Next Friday when he picks you up from training is the opportunity. I am with my grandparents from Friday to help them with the new apartment. There you have to let off steam all night. "

" I don't know. Everything is arranged like that. And somehow ... a little perverse, don't you think? "

"Why?"

"Well, the daughter plans to seduce her father with her best friend, with whom she just had great sex. It's not really normal."

"What is normal. So listen. You dig out your old school uniform, or you borrow one in costume supplies. If I look at the collection above like this, I guess you can get it from Beate Uhse too, or something. You put them on Friday after training at the latest. In addition either a string or better still without. You will of course have to improvise the rest. The small forest car park on the route should be ideal, or stop here, or wherever. You can do that, my old gentleman is only a man, after

all. " " I don't know. I don't feel comfortable with the thought. "

"But it makes you horny, the thought, doesn't it?"

At the word horny she ran a finger through my still wet crease, which I acknowledged with an uncontrolled twitch of my hips. It was extreme.

"Oh god, stop, I can't go on," I squeaked, startled by my own reaction.

"Speaking of awesome, it's me too and you owe me an orgasm. So it's your turn again. I want your tongue deep in my asshole feel."

With these words she sat on my face and I obediently thrust my tongue into her anus.

The End.

# *In the club*

I giggled and closed the apartment door and followed my best friend Nadja into the living room. We left the bags from our shopping tour in the hallway. I let myself down on the soft sofa and took off my shoes.

I sighed in relief and rubbed my aching feet. As so often, the short tour turned into a stroll for hours and I was happy to be able to walk around barefoot.

I looked around for Nadja and called: "Where are you?"

"I'll be right there with you Vicky!" Came her voice from the kitchen.

When she came back from the kitchen, I saw that she had also taken off her shoes and was only wearing her stockings. She held a bottle of champagne in one hand and two glasses in the other. She grinned when she saw that I had made myself as comfortable, sat down with me, opened the bottle and poured us.

She lounged on the sofa next to me and then said: "Cheers, sweetie!"

We clinked glasses and I took my first sip of sparkling wine.

"What does your love life do at all?" Asked Nadja directly after we had only played innocuous small talk while shopping.

I sighed and replied: "I just can't find anyone with whom I can imagine a lasting relationship!"

"And it's not enough for something volatile?" Nadja asked interested.

"Better not!", I admitted honestly, but then added: "But it's been low tide for a long time, right?"

Nadja remained silent and sipped her champagne instead.

I smiled and then said: "We don't look that bad after all, there has to be something going on."

"Should be assumed," agreed Nadja.

"If I don't know if there is anything, I don't want to have the guy at my home, let alone go to him," I said.

"I know what you mean," Nadja agreed, "I met someone the other day ..."

"

"Well, I met him through such a platform," she said apologetically, "I hadn't told you about it because it was so frustrating."

I just nodded and continued listening to Nadja's remarks.

"So we had an appointment in a bar and he was just talking all the time. About his job, his car, his ex-girlfriend - without a period or a comma. I would have left long ago if I hadn't been so horny all the time I was just wondering how to get the guy to shut up and get in the box. "

I took another sip of champagne. I was undeniably touched by Nadja's story.

"In the end I had listened to his life story and invited him to my apartment here. My hope was that he would still do my laundry in the hallway and we would do it on the runner."

"Obviously nothing came of it," I concluded amused.

"But totally! First he looked at my apartment in peace, asked how high the rent is here and praised my taste in furnishings."

I had to laugh unconsciously and poured champagne while Nadja continued to tell her story.

"When I had him here on the sofa and wanted to get to him, he asked me if I could make him a tea because the two cyclists in the bar hit him a bit on the stomach."

Nadja's voice was almost overflowing now and got a shrill undertone.

"That was the final for me. I then shoved him to the door, gave him Maaloxan and then said that I wanted to fuck and not talk to him about the interior or his digestive problems."

Nadja was really in a rage. I only knew her as one of the dearest, most sensitive and warm-hearted people. The guy must have stripped her of all nerves.

She emptied her glass all at once before continuing: "He then described me as an insensitive, horny chick before I slammed the door in front of him."

Amused, I said, "Another reason not to bring the guy home," and poured the two of us.

"Do you remember my vacation flirt that happened to come from our city?" I picked up the thread.

Nadja nodded and listened to what I said.

"I got endless text messages from him and I just thought that he should just write in one sentence the next time we meet. Instead, he literally spammed me at trivial things so I ended it."

"The best thing is to buy a guy who spoils us both," suggested Nadja.

We both laughed and now I realized that I was a little drunk.

"You mean a call boy," I said.

"Exactly! Do you have any idea what it costs?" Came from Nadja.

"You are not serious," I said.

"Why not him? We both have good jobs and are independent," she objected.

"As a woman, I don't pay for sex," I said with a negative gesture, "and I would still have the guy with me."

Nadja thought about it and then it burst out of her: "Tell Vicky, how about we two go to a swinger club?"

"Not serious?" I asked incredulously and started giggling.

"Why not?" Nadja replied and I noticed the look she gave me.

"Neither of us have a boyfriend," I found, "and swinging, which is partner swapping, involves something that can be swapped."

"You can find out more. Would you like to?",

Drunk and slightly excited by the conversation, I said: "Yes, but!"

"But what?" Said Nadja, who was already fired up.

"Then when should we take with us?" I brought up this point that was important to me.

"The two of us just go as a couple," suggested Nadja.

Now I was uncomfortably touched and asked freely: "We have known each other for a relatively long time, but do you like me?"

Nadja laughed cheerfully and wiped a tear away before she answered me with a wink: "Who knows! But actually I'm only looking for someone who will come because I don't trust myself alone."

"You don't have to worry about anything. Let me do it," she offered, "but you don't pinch,

The next day at work, she came to my desk. She looked around conspiratorially and made sure that we were alone before putting a briefcase in front of me.

"What is that?" I asked.

"Look in!" She said.

I opened the folder and saw a sheet with "underneath and over" on it. It was obviously the expression of an advertising flyer from a swinger club.

I looked at Nadja reproachfully and then said: "You hurried to listen!"

"You promised it to me?" She reminded me of my promise.

I looked at her crookedly and reproachfully and said: "I had been drinking too much!"

"Drunk and small children speak the truth. Don't let me hang out Vicky," she begged, looking at me with her big eyes.

"I'm only coming with you because of you," I said, adding: "And I don't let any old, horny goats mount me."

"You don't have to," replied Nadja, "you won't be forced to do anything. And look, they also have a buffet, free drinks and whirlpool."

"What they cost a lot," I said, "I'm really short on cash at the moment, because of the car repair and our shopping tour. I can't afford that at the moment and I don't want to get away from you either be invited. "

Nadja grinned broadly and then said: "That's the best thing about the club. Women without men come in for free."

"That reinforces my thesis with the horny guys," I now gave cause for concern.

"Just think of it as a wellness package", Nadja tempted me and then said, "I also take care of you that nothing happens!"

I gave myself a jerk and then said: "Ok, I promised it!"

"Juhu," triumphed Nadja, "I'll pick you up around eight on Saturday!"

To my surprise, Nadja was also on time for a change. I got in and drove her to the club, which was a little out of the way on the edge of the city forest.

"For the fact that you have no desire, you made yourself well," Nadja teased, who was driving the car and only glanced over at me.

Instead of answering, I just smiled.

I was wearing my short dress, which was slit so high on the side and emphasized my figure. Plus lingerie and high shoes. It had taken a little effort, but I had also shaved my pussy so that I could feel the silk fabric of my panties comfortably in my crotch. I knew that Nadja never went on a date unshaven. So I didn't want to be stuck in front of her. To my surprise, Nadja only showed up with my shirt and jeans. She had her black hair tied in a ponytail. On the other hand, I had my red mane nicely coiffed and felt a little overdressed next to her.

We parked in front of a building in front of which was a sign that read "Drunter & Druber". Hedges surrounded the actual building, so that little could be seen except for the roof of the house. The path under the sign led to the entrance door, which had no knob but only a knob. Nadja rang the doorbell next to the door and a few moments later a lady in an attractive dress opened it to us.

"Hello you two sweeties," she greeted us and asked us inside.

Through the semitransparent dress of the lady you could see her very tight underwear.

She looked us over and asked, "Are you a couple?"

We looked at each other questioningly.

"I had heard that women have free access, so is it important that we are together?" I asked, unsettled.

"Not that," the lady replied with a cheeky grin, "but then I was interested and you would make a great couple."

We looked at each other again and had to smile.

"It's your first time here, right?" She asked and we nodded.

"So I'm Petra," she said, "we're all here with you and they're all super nice. If there is anything, you can contact me at any time. There is not much going on at the moment. Most people come later. Then it's fuller here too. "

We both nodded shyly, like little schoolgirls.

However, Petra smiled it away gently and continued: "Eat and drink as much as you want. Be polite but do not let yourself be pushed to anything you do not want. There are enough condoms and towels in every room. Use both abundantly."

She looked at us and asked, "Anything unclear?"

"I don't think so," I said, looking at Nadja.

"Everything is clear with me," she replied.

"Now you two sweeties," said Petra, "here is the changing room. I wish you a lot of fun and ask quietly if you want to know something."

She showed us the way and went back to the entrance. Nadja and I made our way to the changing rooms.

The way there led past the bar. Contrary to my guess, it was more of a sauna club, since the guests mostly sat there with a towel or bathrobe folded over. So unlike Nadja, I was really overdressed.

Passing the bar, the two of us already drew the admiring glances of the men and some women. Nadja clearly enjoyed it and was in no real hurry. I couldn't help myself from the charm of this situation.

Arrived in the locker room, Nadja immediately undressed. Under the shirt she was not wearing a bra, which she rarely needed for her small breasts, and when she unbuttoned and pulled off the jeans I saw her hairless slit between the legs.

"Go ahead, dare Vicky," she teased me.

I smiled painedly and opened the fasteners on my dress. During this time other guests of the club came, who greeted us warmly, quickly undressed and then disappeared again.

I gathered all my courage, opened my bra and pulled down my panties. Now it was me who lured Nadja out of the reserve when she saw my shaved pussy and let out an appreciative whistle. I thanked me with a slight nod.

Large towels were stacked on a table. Nadja took two and passed one of them to me, which I quickly wrapped up before I let anyone see more than I wanted.

"You have great breasts," said Nadja suddenly.

"Excuse me?" I replied, completely out of the concept.

Nadja and I had known each other since school and although we started different apprenticeships, we met again later at work. Nadja knew how I look naked and the other way around as well. That is why I was so unsettled by her statement.

"Oh! Thanks!" I replied flattered and slightly confused.

Nadja laughed cheerfully and then said: "I want to go to the sauna! Are you coming with me?"

I nodded and followed her. The signage led us directly to a sauna hut in the garden. I was annoyed with myself that I was so scared and shy and that only Nadja was running after me. That needs to change. I overtook her, opened the sauna door, and entered. Now Nadja had to follow me. As she closed the door behind me, I was already looking over the people present.

I threw a nice "evening" in the round, which was also returned. The eyes of the mostly male sauna-goers were focused on us two newcomers.

I enjoyed loosening the towel and then slowly sliding down my curves. I put the towel over an empty spot on the wooden bench and sat on it.

The gentlemen's attention was now certain to me and I thought to myself: "People! Just look, don't touch!"

Nadja sat down next to me and it wasn't long before the sweat ran from our pores and I brushed it off my breasts. Upon entering I had already looked at the large hourglass and after more than 10 minutes found that it was time to go again.

"I'm going out again," I told Nadja.

"I'm coming with you," she agreed, and we rose.

Soaked in sweat, we crossed the stone path back to the house and turned towards the showers. However, there were no individual wet rooms or shower heads. There was a room with benches and wall hooks from which you could see the shower room. There were several heads attached to the ceiling and a crowd of people of both sexes huddled under it, as there were more people willing to shower than shower heads.

I looked at Nadja questioningly. She shrugged her shoulders, hung her towel on the hook and moved in the crowd of people taking a shower. I regretted at the moment that I had put so much effort into my hair because it would stick to me wet anyway. So I did the same to Nadja and followed her. I washed the sweat from my body and could not avoid occasionally feeling a hand on my ass or breasts and touching bare skin myself. I tried to keep the showering process as short as possible, already dried myself off and tied my hair together when Nadja also left the shower.

"It's great in the shower," she said cheerfully, "and there are even two birds in the corner!"

But with a little interest I stretched my neck and saw a woman with her arms and legs wrapped around her supposed partner, who pressed her to the wall of the shower. Rhythmically pushed his pelvis forward and on her hot look I saw that he was doing it well for her.

I smiled, envied the couple for so much shamelessness and started rubbing myself with body lotion, which was available here for everyone.

"Do you want too?" I asked Nadja and held out the bottle, which she gratefully accepted.

I continued to apply cream and took my time because I noticed how more and more men came to watch us. In the meantime, I didn't care that I was naked. I enjoyed the looks of desire that rested on me and Nadja also enjoyed the game we were playing here.

"Cream each other," someone called a lustful suggestion and another asked, "Should I put cream on you?"

I looked at Nadja and bit my lower lip indecisively. I was already tempted to heat up the gentlemen present. Before I could make a  decision, she pulled me close and started rubbing her creamy breasts on mine. I felt the hard buds of her small firm breasts, sighed with delight and wondered if Nadja had hoped more from accompanying me here.

I took the bottle, put something on my hand and started to apply more cream to Nadja. I spread the white milk on her body, taking my time and not skipping her thighs. Nadja moaned briefly when I brushed her column.

Now it was my turn and enjoyed how she kneaded and caressed my breasts while applying cream. Her hand gently stroked my flat stomach and bluntly disappeared between my thighs, causing me to gasp and feel goose bumps.

If Nadja had gone on now, I would have allowed it. But now she went back to innocuous stroking. So I looked around the room and saw what was happening around us.

Our small insert had obviously had an effect on the women and men present. The men's cocks were sometimes hard erected and some women played with their pussy without shame.

Unfortunately there was no man who agreed with me. I went through them one by one and found something to complain about. Too big, too small, too fat, bald, small tail. There was always something that bothered me. I was already wondering whether my demands weren't too high.

I ended the game with Nadja, wrapped the towel around me again and saw some disappointed looks from our spectators who turned to other things.

I looked at Nadja and asked: "I'm going to the bar. Are you coming with sweetie?"

"Go ahead, I'll come over," she said, and I couldn't miss the lustful look she gave one of the men who was watching us.

"Seriously?" I asked.

"Let's see, I think he's cute," she said, walking lasciviously towards him.

I smiled and left the room. The bar was right near the showers. I sat down and ordered a cocktail. One wouldn't hurt. I knew what alcohol had on me, but now I wanted to have a drink. I told the bartender not to put so much alcohol in. After I sipped on the straw and felt the sweet, fruity taste on my tongue, I knew that it would be difficult to leave it with one.

On the other hand, I didn't want to give myself up drunk to anyone I soberly refused. I sighed, took a long sip of my drink, and watched the other guests.

A passage from the bar led into an area that Petra hadn't shown us anymore and which giggled into the more frequent couples. The whole thing made me curious. I took my glass, held the large tied towel with my other hand, and followed them.

Behind the passage was a jumble of corridors and rooms with play areas that alternated thematically.

Several couples kissed and caressed each other on these playgrounds and I wondered how many of the ladies had only met their lover here and today. Many already had sex and didn't let the people around them bother them in the least. A young woman greedily rode her lover. She had thrown her head back excitedly and moaned voluptuously in my direction. I saw her firm ass and her  lover's big cock plunging deep into her.

I got warm and my pussy started to tingle, I broke away from the scene and went to another room where two women were in the center of several men and more and more were added. They alternately let the men fuck and fondle them, spoiling one or more with their mouths.

A shiver ran down my spine. At the same time, I was fascinated and couldn't take my eyes off. My free hand slid under the towel and I groaned as I rubbed my column with my hand.

"Come on! There's still room for you," one of the participants who had noticed me invited me and tore me out of my thoughts.

This invitation was also friendly and as if he had invited me for a nice chat with friends. I lifted my hand, which I had drawn out from under the towel, smiled and went back to the bar, hoping to find Nadja there. However, it was not to be seen. She wasn't in the shower either.

I sighed, went back to the bar and sat on one of the chairs and put down my empty glass.

"Do you want another cocktail?" Asked the friendly bartender.

"Gladly!" I replied and thought: "A second won't hurt!"

While I sipped the new drink, a small bald man came to me. He was fat and had the towel tied around his waist.

"Is there a free place here?",

I moved up a little and let him sit in the chair next to me.

"Can I invite you for a drink?" He continued.

"The drinks are free," I replied amused, "it is difficult to invite them."

"Uh, sure," he said, and I grinned inwardly that I could get him out of the way so easily.

"Are you here more often?", He continued to dig.

"No, for the first time!" I replied uninterested.

I wondered how I could get rid of him without bumping him in the head because he didn't seem to understand that I wasn't interested.

"Shouldn't we go back and I'll show you everything?" He offered himself now.

"I'm sorry, I'm not interested in you," I now made it clear.

I tried to smile at him kindly but firmly.

The gentleman nodded a little disappointed and said: "Then not! Still a lot of fun."

I was sorry to disappoint people every time. For me, this led me to go far. So I got up, took my glass and wanted to go. Without seeing where I was going, I bumped into another man and spilled part of my cocktail.

"Sorry!" I asked, looking in when I ran in there.

There was a big guy in front of me. Striking face carved out of rock and a three-day beard. He had a towel tied around his waist. He was muscular and strong.

"You should see where you're going," growled his deep voice.

I've always loved men with a deep voice.

I thought I felt the deep bass even in my pussy and said: "I'm sorry!"

But he didn't seem upset, but gave me a warm, friendly smile.

"Where did the young Merida go to?" He asked, amused.

I knew he was referring to my red hair, but I couldn't find the words, so I answered without thinking: "Backwards!"

He laughed friendly and then said: "All alone? But you're brave."

Now I was back and answered flirtatiously: "Then I need a protector to defend me!"

"I'm happy to do that," he said, offering me his strong arm.

I took the offered arm and followed it through the passage to the rooms. Together we explored this area and when I heard a groan from a room that seemed familiar to me, I let go of his arm and took a look.

I saw Nadja kneeling on all fours, blowing a man's cock in front and from behind she let the guy fuck her from the shower.

"She didn't take much time," I thought to myself, wondering how she had passed the bar unseen when my companion tore me out of my thoughts.

"Do you like that?" He asked.

"I don't know! I think so," I admitted and was fascinated that my girlfriend was so willing to take me.

"Have you tried?" He asked.

"No!" I replied horrified.

"Then you can't say whether you like it," he said with a smile, "you should just give it a try."

I briefly watched the scene in front of me. Nadja turned her head and looked directly at me. Her look suggested how much pleasure the two gentlemen were giving her. She smiled and then put her mouth over the tail in front of her again.

I broke away from the sight and said to my companion: "Let's go on!"

"Where should it go, beautiful flower," he wanted to know.

The path led us into a larger room, in the middle of which was an elevated couch that stood like an altar in the room.

I felt his hand on my ass and protested, "Hey!"

"You said that I should decide and you wanted to try something," he said temptingly.

I felt a wetness appear between my thighs that grew stronger than his other hand caressed one of my breasts with the towel and nipped my rebellion in the bud. I sighed with delight. With his hand on my ass, he picked me up and laid me on the couch.

He brushed the towel off my body, looked at my naked body and grunted contentedly.

He leaned forward to reach my breasts and started sucking on one of my buds and kissing them. This straightened up immediately and the woolly feeling of excitement started from there towards my lap. When I felt his demanding hand in my crotch, I was briefly startled, but then opened my thighs willingly as he began to caress me tenderly.

His hand brushed my side from my breasts. Past my hip, down my thighs and up the inside again, up to my gate. When he entered me with a finger, I felt how wet I was already.

"Everything OK," I thought to myself, closed my eyes and let me caress him, "and if he goes too far for you, you just say stop!"

His kisses went deeper and deeper. I groaned and gasped as his rough tongue reached my pleasure pearl and lingered there. Hands massaged my breasts and I enjoyed these touches. I felt my nipples suck as he continued to lick me and I realized we were no longer alone.

I kept my eyes closed and didn't dare to see who owned those tongues that danced around my nipples because it was just too beautiful and I let myself go to my head cinema.

I heard the crackle of a condom that was unpacked and, like in a trance, I registered someone grabbing my legs and pushing them back. Shortly afterwards I felt something slide up and down my wet column. I groaned with lust and it wasn't long before the one who increased the pressure penetrated deep into me and stretched my soaking wet cunt. I gave a short cry of pleasure when I was taken so unexpectedly. Slowly he started to move inside me, carefully increasing the speed and when he noticed that I was moving towards him willingly, he started to fuck me passionately. I unexpectedly noticed how a second cock bumped against my lips. I opened my mouth, let it go, sucked, licked and took it deep in my mouth.

My cunt, which was abstaining for far too long, greedily took up the hard cock of my lover, who now thrust me powerfully and deeply. Moaning with lust, I tried not to neglect the tail in my mouth at the same time. While both hard cocks dipped into both of my body openings, a nimble tongue pampered my sensitive lust pearl, so that it didn't take long for an orgasm of enormous proportions to sweep through my body. My pussy twitched, clung to the tail, which  became significantly thicker at that moment and I heard a relieved groan above me. He pushed his cock deep into me again before sliding out of me. I was not surprised when another cock took its place shortly after and continued to fuck me.

I felt almost a dozen hands on me and I still kept my eyes closed, afraid that the dream would burst. The tails continued to change in mouth and cunt. I drove the pictures of the men from the shower in my head from one climax to the next and I was sure that one or the other of these men had already fucked me. Contrary to my initial rejection, it created an unexpected pleasure in me and gave me a delight that I bluntly moaned out.

A shiver of pleasure came over me when a skillful tongue dipped into my cunt.

"Is that cool," I groaned and pushed myself towards my patron.

At the same time I dared to open my eyes again. Various men and women were still with me, stroking and kissing me. I seemed to have become the center of a big lovemaking. I saw some men lying a little apart, who were visibly satisfied, the condoms still over their sagging tails, filled with their semen.

My big partner who had brought me here already seemed to be gone. I groaned when the demanding tongue hit my irritated pleasure button again and looked down.

There I discovered Nadja, who was kneeling between my spread thighs and licking myself with devotion. My eyes sparkled with lust and I groaned again as she rolled her tongue around my pearl.

Smacking, she parted from my pussy and said: "You see Vicky, it was worth it for you too."

Instead of answering, I just nodded and saw how one of the gentlemen present, who had not yet been on the train, put on a condom behind Nadja. He briefly tapped Nadja, who immediately understood, dropped to her knees and stretched her ass towards the gentleman while she continued to lick my cunt.

I looked her straight in the eye as the man took her in front of me from behind. The lust glittered out of her eyes. Nadja groaned with pleasure and then closed it with pleasure.

The End.